It's the annual Adopt-a-Dog Fair at Puppy Haven Park. On this special day, puppies dogs gather in the park to meet their new families. come to the fair hoping to find a new furry friend to take home.

Duke is a frisky, happy golden retriever puppy. Today his fur is brushed and he's wearing his finest bandana. He's very excited and wants to look his best when he finds his new family.

Duke's good friends are also at the
Adopt-a-Dog Fair. They are looking for new families, too.

George is a big, strong German shepherd.
Polly is a poodle with fur as white as cotton balls.
Dotty is a Dalmatian with black spots all over.

The good friends are happy to see each other and
wag their tails. Duke wants to run and play, but his friends
say, "No way!" They want to stay neat and clean when
meeting the people who are coming to the fair.

Dog & Puppy
Adoption
Here Today

3

On the other side of the park

Jay Bush is looking for a new puppy pal. Jay wants to find a dog to bring home to the Bush's family farm. This morning Jay carefully combed his hair and dressed in his favorite shirt. He wants to look his best when he finds his new furry friend.

Jay is worried though, because he has looked and looked, but he still hasn't found a dog to adopt. He wonders if he will find a dog who wants to come home to the farm with him.

There are many people at the fair, and Duke looks and looks for just the right person to adopt him. Soon his friends are all very happy because they have found new families.

George finds a police officer who was looking for a big dog with a deep, loud bark. Polly finds a family with a little girl who likes to dress up and have make-believe tea parties. Dotty finds a firefighter who wants a dog to go for rides on his big red truck.

Duke is happy for
them, but he wonders who
will want a playful puppy who
likes to run and have fun?
Then, Duke looks across the park and
his ears perk up.

He sees Jay, the Bush's Baked Beans guy!

Jay is wearing a shirt with exactly the same pattern as Duke's bandana. Duke just knows that he and Jay will make a perfect new family.

Duke starts to run toward Jay. He doesn't see Mr. Periwinkle, who is carrying a big plate of yummy food. Mr. Periwinkle trips and his plate lands on the fancy hat of Mrs. Noodle-Doodle. Mrs. Noodle-Doodle jumps up and accidentally knocks over the table sending little Sally Sandpiper flying onto the dessert table, where she lands in a batch of delicious fruit pies.

The pies fly everywhere. A lemon meringue pie lands right on Jay's head!

Duke finally catches up to Jay and licks his face.

"Did you do all this, little dog?" laughs Jay. Duke and Jay both know they'll be a perfect match. Duke climbs into Jay's truck and barks his good-bye to his friends. He and Jay drive home.

When they get to the Bush's family farm, Duke can't believe his eyes. There are big fields where he can run. There is a big barn where he can hide in the hay. After Duke has a dinner of his favorite dog food, he even finds his very own dog bed where he can sleep.

Jay says, "Get a good night's sleep, little Duke. Tomorrow we'll have a busy day." Then he tucks Duke into the big snuggly dog bed.

Duke learns that there is much work to do on a bean farm and each day is very busy. There are animals to feed, cleaning to be done, and beans to tend. Each season brings new jobs to do.

In the summer the beans need lots of water. Duke likes to splash in the water.

In the fall there are lots of leaves to rake. Duke likes to play in the leaves.

In the winter there is snow to shovel. Duke likes to make tracks in the snow.

Through each season, Duke gets bigger and stronger and more mischievous.

As Duke gets older it is his job to chase rabbits out of the field because rabbits love to eat bean plants. Duke shoos them away, back into their rabbit dens.

The rabbits always come back and Duke shoos them away again. It's very important to be sure the bean plants grow big and strong.

Duke's favorite trick is to hide Jay's eyeglasses. If Jay doesn't have his glasses his vision is blurry.

"Oh, Duke! Not again!" Jay laughs when he realizes his glasses are missing. He always finds his glasses after a few minutes of searching.

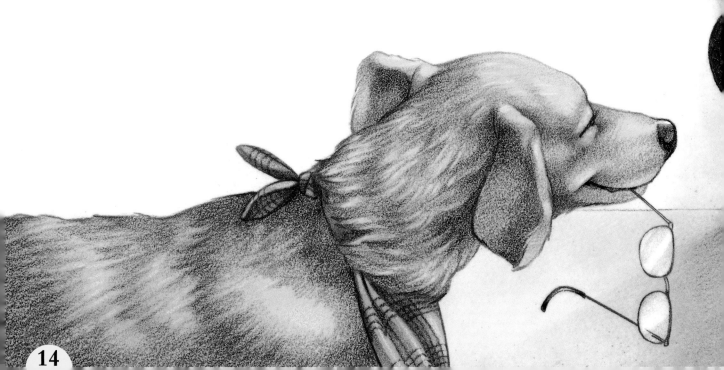

While Duke loves everything about the farm, he loves chasing rabbits most of all.

Duke chases rabbits out of the field.

Duke chases rabbits out of the barn.

Duke chases rabbits back into their rabbit dens.

Even though this is an important job, both Duke and the rabbits love playing this chasing game.

There is one place on the farm where Duke is not allowed to chase rabbits. This is a big bean silo where the harvested beans are stored. It is very tall and holds many beans high up in the air.

Duke is not allowed to go near the silo. It is not a safe place for young dogs to run or work or play.

One bright sunny day, Jay is working near the silo, tinkering with his tractor. Duke is in the bean field looking for rabbits.

While Jay works, one of those pesky rabbits hops out of the barn, into one side of the tractor, then out the other side of the tractor, landing on the release lever for the silo!

Suddenly,

a flood of beans pours out of the silo!

The beans pour and pour.

Before Jay can move, they're
as high as his waist.

More and more beans pour out of
the silo door. Quick as a flash, Jay is covered in beans
up to his shoulders.

Jay calls out, "Duke! Help me get out of
this bean pile!"

Duke hears Jay's call and runs
over to the silo. He sees Jay
covered in beans.

"Thank goodness you're here, Duke! Help me get out of here," says Jay.

Duke wags his tail and climbs up the pile of beans to lick Jay's face. Jay laughs.

"Come on, Duke! That tickles!" he says.

Jay realizes he forgot to say the magic word. "Okay, Duke – *please* help me out of here!"

Duke starts to dig. He is now a big, strong dog, and he digs and digs into the bean pile. Soon, Jay is free, but the beans are scattered everywhere.

There are beans all over the ground. There are beans on the tractor. Jay even has beans in his pockets!

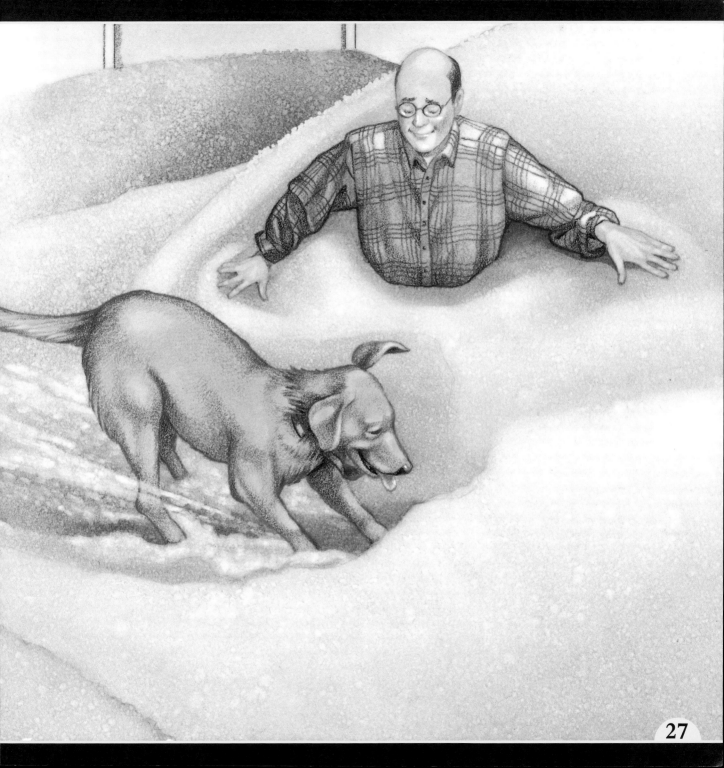

Jay smiles at Duke and says, "Duke, this is one mess I'm *glad* you made! Thank you for saving me. I'm so lucky to have such a good and loyal friend."

From that day on, Duke is allowed to go anywhere on the farm – even near the silo.

That night, Jay and Duke finish their dinner and relax on the porch, looking out over the sunset. They both feel very happy and content.

Jay puts his arm around Duke and says, "Duke, you're my best friend. One day soon, I'll tell you a very important family secret. But for now, it's time for good friends to say good night."

To Be Continued...

Copyright © 2006 Bush Brothers & Company

For more information visit www.bushbeans.com/dukestails

Published by Bush Brothers & Company
1016 East Weisgarber Road
Knoxville, TN 37909-2683

Publisher's Cataloging-in-Publication Data

Duke finds a home / story by Duke ; illustrations by Rob Lawson. - Knoxville, TN :
Bush Bros. & Co., 2006.

31 p. : ill. ; cm. (Duke's tails)
ISBN: 0-9779308-0-7
ISBN 13: 978-0-9779308-0-7

1. Dog adoption-Juvenile fiction. 2. Friendship-Juvenile fiction. I. Duke. II. Lawson, Rob, ill.
III. Title.

SF427.D85   2006902017
                    [E]-dc22

Book production and coordination by Jenkins Group, Inc.
www.BookPublishing.com
Interior design: Eric Tufford
Cover design: Chris Rhoads
Illustrations: Rob Lawson

Printed in Canada
10 09 08 07 06 • 5 4 3 2 1